TWENTY-TWO, TWENTY-THREE

1

TWENTY-TWO,

Welcome to
TITLE PAGE

2

ELLEN RASKIN

TWENTY-THREE

ATHENEUM, NEW YORK

You are now leaving
TITLE PAGE

3

LIBRARY OF CONGRESS CATALOGING IN PUBLICATION DATA

Raskin, Ellen. Twenty-two, twenty-three.
SUMMARY: All the animals have advice for mouse
on what to wear and what not to wear for
the special holiday greeting on Twenty-two, Twenty-three.
[1. Mice—Fiction 2. Animals—Fiction] I. Title.
PZ7.R1817Tw [E] 76-5475 ISBN 0-689-30529-X

Copyright © 1976 by Ellen Raskin

Published simultaneously in Canada by McClelland & Stewart, Ltd.
Manufactured in the United States of America
Printed by Connecticut Printers, Inc., Hartford, Connecticut
Bound by A. Horowitz & Son/Bookbinders, Clifton, New Jersey

FIRST EDITION

4

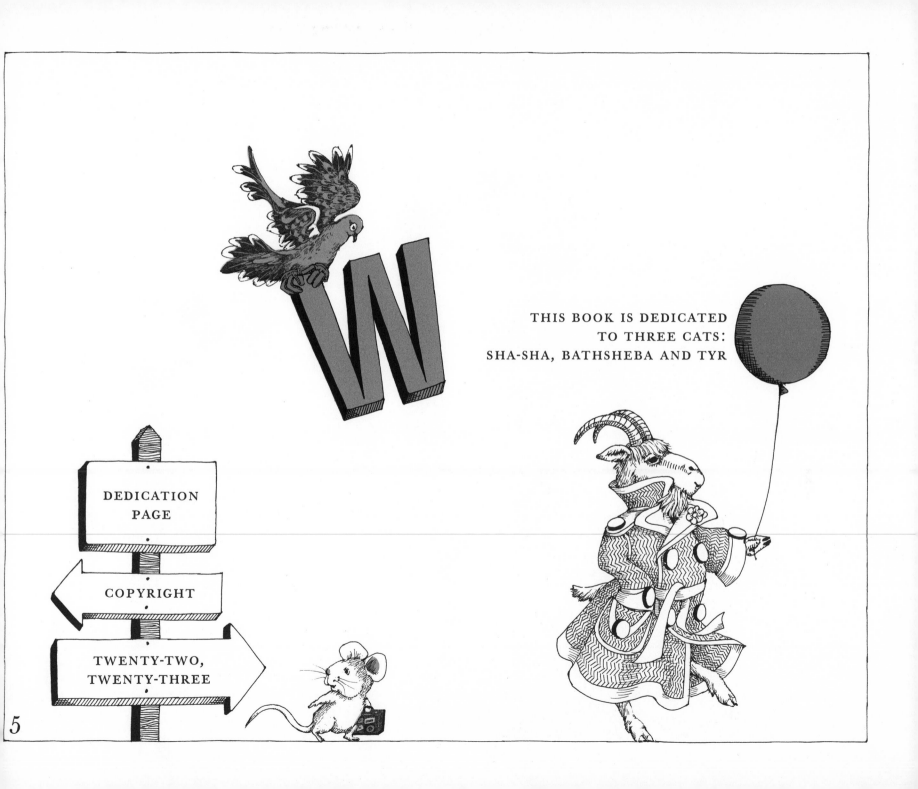

THIS BOOK IS DEDICATED
TO THREE CATS:
SHA-SHA, BATHSHEBA AND TYR

6

"Pardon me,"
said the traveling mouse,
"but what is this
and where are we?"

"It is not where we are,"
said the ape in the cape,
said the goat in the coat,
"it is where
and what
we are going to be."

"Below and above,"
said the dove
with gloves on his feet.

"Here and there,"
  said the bear in his underwear.

  Said the gibbons in ribbons,
"Up in the air."

"Down in a hole,"
  said the gopher in the loafer.

8

"Down in a hole,"
said the mole in the stole.

"Twenty-two, Twenty-three,"
said the dove
with gloves on his feet.

9

10

Oh, this mouse had been
almost everywhere, but never
to Twenty-two, Twenty-three.
"May I come, too?" said she.

"Absolutely not,"
said the cock in the smock,
said the fox in socks.

"You are naked, madame,"
said the ram in the tam.

Said the snail in the veil,
"Off, off to jail."

"Get dressed, my love,"
said the dove
with gloves on his feet.

Quickly the mouse put on a muumuu.
"Now may I come with you?"

"Not in that,"
said the owl in the cowl,
said the yak in the sack.

"A mouse in a muumuu cannot be
on Twenty-two or Twenty-three,"
said the cat in the hat.

"Change, muumuu-ed mouse,"
said the dove
with gloves on his feet.

Poor mouse.
Nothing in her wardrobe
seemed to please
these fussy folk.

"Your skirt has shrunk,"
said the rabbit in habit,
said the skunk in trunks.

"A mouse in a tutu will not do
for Twenty-three or Twenty-two,"
said the 'gator in gaiters.

Said the bongos in bows,
"What silly, frilly clothes."

"Change, tutu-ed mouse,"
said the dove
with gloves on his feet.

16

"A sarong does not belong
on Twenty-two,"
said the stilt in kilts.

"A parka is wrong,
quite wrong for you,"
said the pig in the wig.

Said the llama in pajamas,
"Go home to your mouse mama."

"Wait, sweet mate,"
said the dove
with gloves on his feet.

17

"A sari is no better,"
said the setter in the sweater.

"Such frumpy togs,"
said the frogs in clogs.

Said the asses in glasses,
"Indeed.
Besides, we have plenty;
we have much too many
for Twenty-two, Twenty-three."

"A little mouse takes little room
—in the right costume,"
said the dove
with gloves on his feet.

18

19

Off flew the dove
with the sari in his gloves
and draped it on the sloth.
Said the sloth in cloth,
"The mouse may stay."

"Hooray," said everybody,
"the mouse in the blouse
may stay."

"Hooray for me," said the mouse in the blouse, "for I'm on my way to Twenty-two, Twenty-three."

"On your toes," said the turtle in the kirtle.

"Assume your pose," said the does in hose.

"Now, somebody, somewhere, please turn the page," said the dove with gloves on his feet.

HAPPY CHRISTMAS

from page Twenty-two
said the ape in the cape,
the cat in the hat,
the yak in the sack,
the bongos in bows,
the stilt in kilts,
the gopher in the loafer,
the snail in the veil,
the owl in the cowl,
the 'gator in gaiters,
the frogs in clogs,
the llama in pajamas,
the ram in the tam,
the goat in the coat,
and the bear
in his underwear.

22

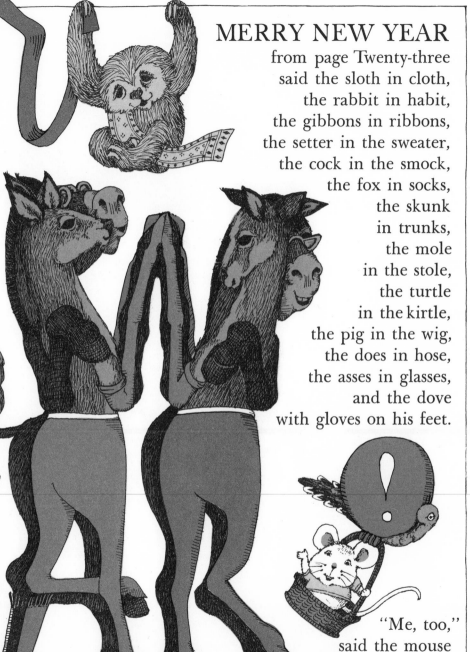

MERRY NEW YEAR
from page Twenty-three
said the sloth in cloth,
the rabbit in habit,
the gibbons in ribbons,
the setter in the sweater,
the cock in the smock,
the fox in socks,
the skunk
in trunks,
the mole
in the stole,
the turtle
in the kirtle,
the pig in the wig,
the does in hose,
the asses in glasses,
and the dove
with gloves on his feet.

"Me, too,"
said the mouse
in the blouse.

"What a nice place to visit,"
said the mouse in the blouse.
"Perhaps I'll come this way again."

"Perhaps we will,"
said the dove
with gloves on his feet.

24

ENDPAPER

BACK COVER

BOOK JACKET

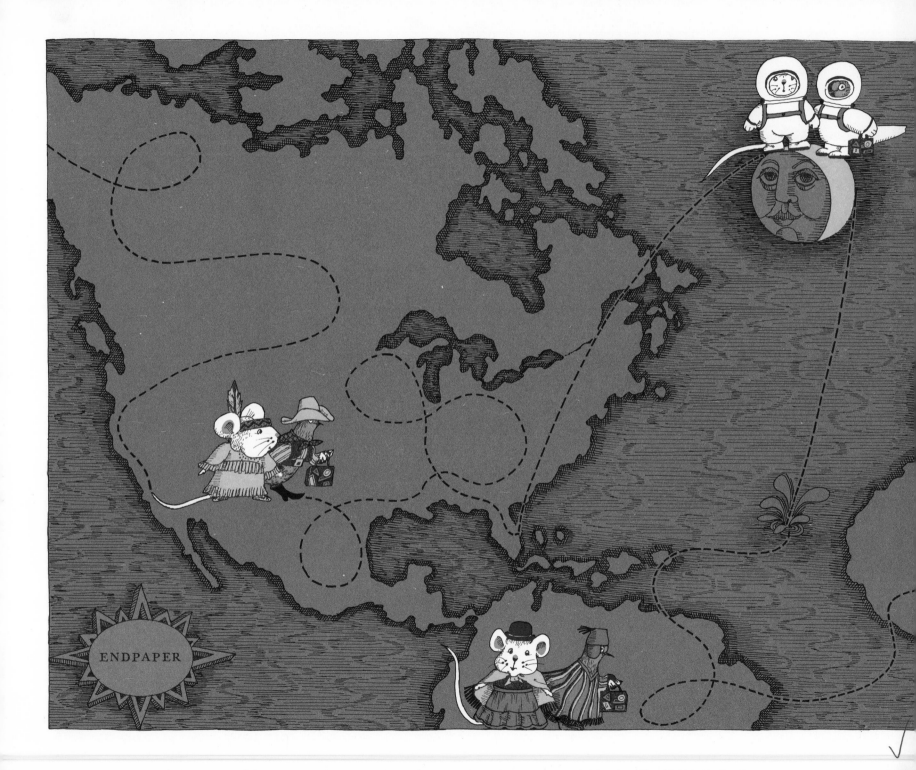

ENDPAPER